T'WIT T'WOO!

Maddy McClellan

meadowside
CHILDREN'S BOOKS

Owls in the kitchen,

Owls in the hall,

Owls playing
with my shoes,

Owls big and small.

Owls on
the rooftops,

Owls in the dark,

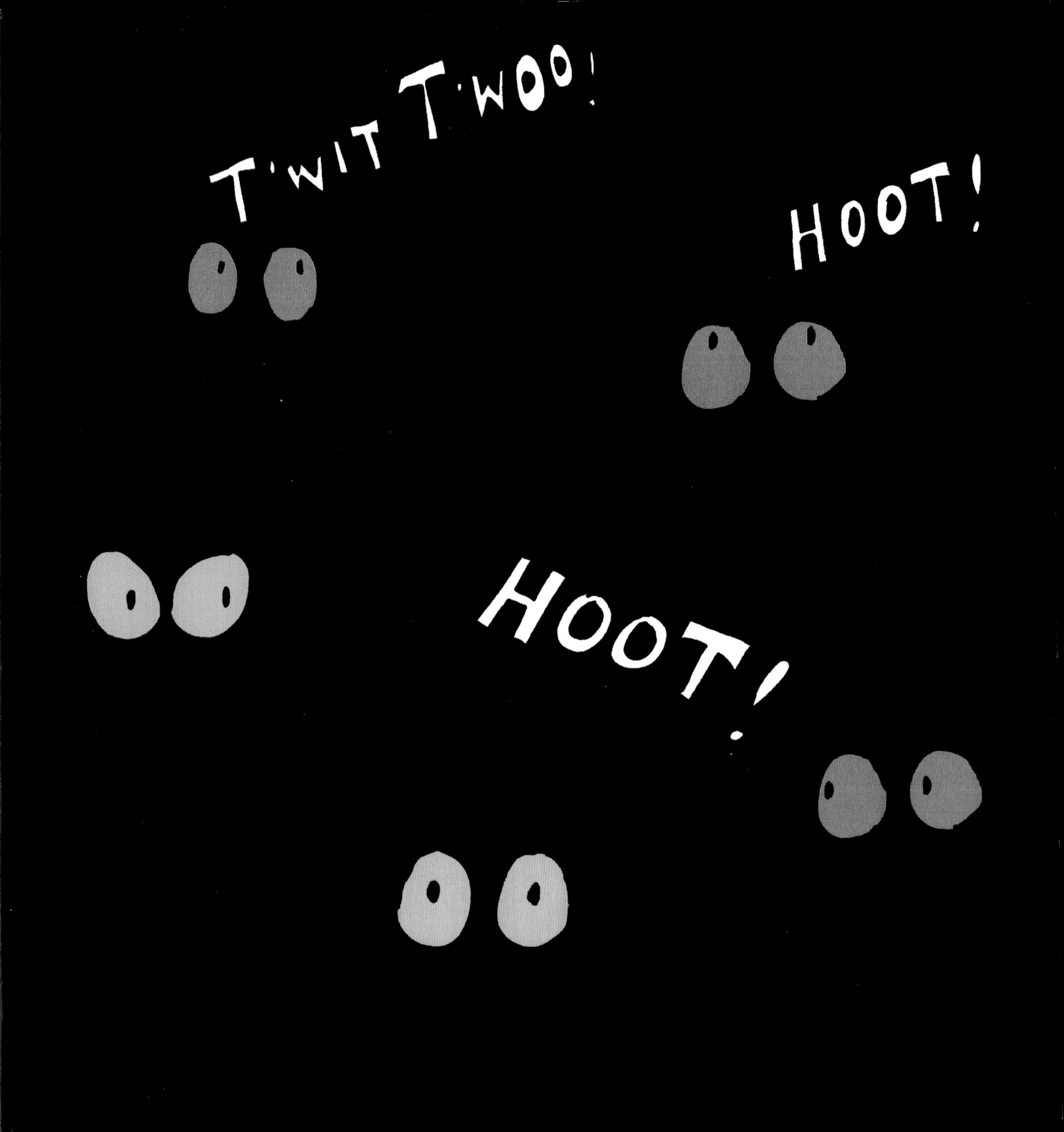
T'WIT T'WOO!
HOOT!
HOOT!

Owls painting
pretty pictures,

Owls in the park.

Owls reading lots of books,
Owls without a care…

Owls having hoots of fun,

TOOT!

Owls everywhere!

For
*Jon and baby Inigo
and of course Ronnie and Ruthie.*

M.M.

First published in 2005
by Meadowside Children's Books
185 Fleet Street, London, EC4A 2HS.

Illustrations © Maddy McClellan, 2005

The right of Maddy McClellan to be identified
as the illustrator of this
work has been asserted by her in
accordance with the Copyright,
Designs and Patents Act, 1988

A CIP catalogue record for this book
is available from the British Library.
Printed in U.A.E.

10 9 8 7 6 5 4 3 2 1